To my husband, Ron, and the entire Poplos and Thompson families. Opa!

- Nicole Poplos Thompson

www.mascotbooks.com

For more information, please contact:
Mascot Books
560 Herndon Parkway #120
Herndon, VA 20170
info@mascotbooks.com

Library of Congress Control Number: 2012942573

CPSIA Code: PRT0213A
ISBN-10: 1620860465
ISBN-13: 9781620860465

Printed in the United States

Sophia Discovers

Occupational Therapy

Nicole Poplos Thompson
illustrated by
Doina Paraschiv

Note to Reader

Being an occupational therapist is great! If you are creative, enjoy working with people, and helping people, it is a very rewarding career. OTs work with babies, kids, teens, and adults. OTs practice in schools, hospitals, rehab centers, skilled nursing facilities, out-patient clinics, and home healthcare.

- Nicole Poplos Thompson

On a chilly November morning, Sophia was eating breakfast at home when her mom shared some exciting news. "Your Greek grandparents are on their way here to Ohio. They're going to celebrate Christmas with the whole Papadopoulos family! Papou and Yiayia are even bringing their favorite donkey, Dimitrios."

Sophia ran next door where her aunt, uncle, and cousins lived. She couldn't wait to spread the news! Sophia announced, "Yiayia and Papou Papadopoulos left their village in Santorini, Greece, and will be here for Christmas!" Her aunt and uncle, Thea Elaine and Theo Jimmy, looked at their sons Nicholas, Gregory, and Andrew. Everyone had huge grins and they all shouted, "Opa!"

Sophia's older cousin, Nicholas, told her that since she was the youngest, Papou was sure to ask her a very important question. Imitating Papou's Greek accent, Nicholas said, "What do you want to be, Sophia, when up you grow?"

Sophia felt nervous and didn't know what she was going to say. She had no idea what she wanted to be. Would she tell Papou she wanted to be an astronaut? A dancer? A veterinarian? Sophia wished she knew what she wanted to be when she grew up.

Meanwhile, the snow was falling and the roads were covered with ice. Sophia kept looking out the window. She wanted to be the first to see Yiayia, Papou, and Dimitrios. For the longest time, all she saw were big snowflakes and the snowman she and her cousins had made to welcome their Greek grandparents to Ohio.

Finally, Sophia heard a *clip* and a *clop*. She knew it had to be Dimitrios! Sophia saw Yiayia and Papou coming down the street. Sophia told the Papadopoulos family, "I see them! If Yiayia brings us a blueberry pie, this will be the best day of my life!" Sophia's mom and dad, Thea Elaine, Theo Jimmy, Nicholas, Gregory, and Andrew all agreed, "Opa!"

Dimitrios tried to stop at the end of the driveway but he was slipping and sliding and could not stop. Dimitrios spun around, his legs going every which way, and landed flat on his tummy!

Yiayia kept her balance as she clutched her blueberry pie. Papou was right behind Yiayia when she started slipping and sliding. Her body flew backward, knocking Papou down. Yiayia was lying on the driveway and Papou rolled down to the street. You don't want to know what happened to the blueberry pie! *Splat!*

Yiayia cried, "Oh dear, I think I broke my hip!"

Papou said, "I cut me lip and bumped me head!"

Dimitrios was not hurt and was busy lapping up the blueberry pie. He transported Papou and Yiayia to the hospital. The doctor told the family, "Yiayia had surgery and got a new hip. Papou has stitches for his lip and head."

The Papadopoulos family went into Yiayia and Papou's hospital room. Yiayia could not walk or get out of bed. She said, "I'm afraid I won't be able to make pies for a very long time."

Sophia saw a bandage on Papou's head. She asked him, "Papou, do you remember my name?"

Papou guessed, "Andrea? Maria? Anna? I think me want to ask you a question but me no remember the question." Sophia was discouraged that Papou did not know her name. But, she was secretly glad he did not ask her what she wanted to be when she grew up. Everyone started to worry the Papadopoulos family Christmas would not happen.

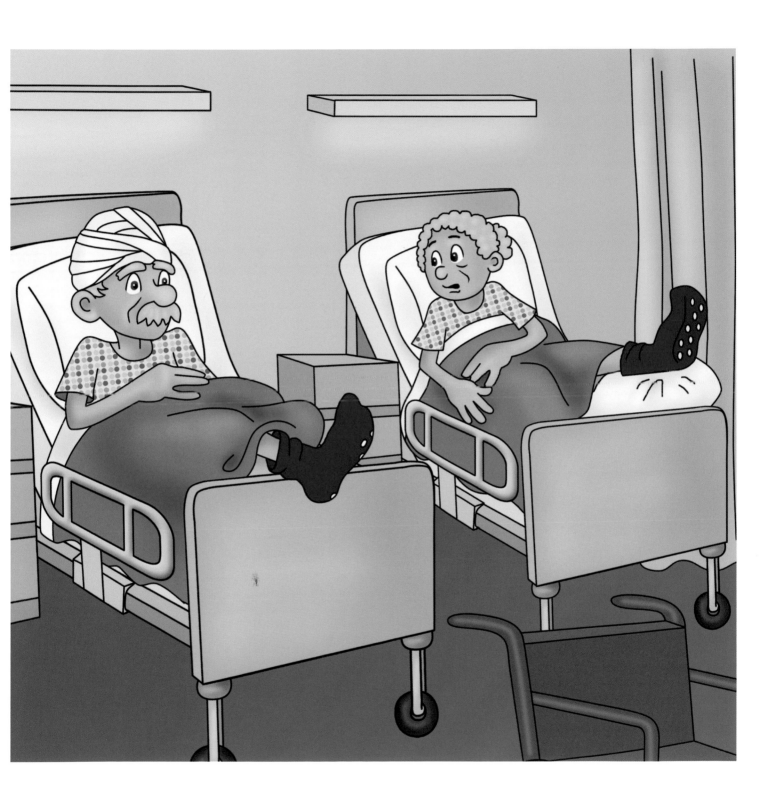

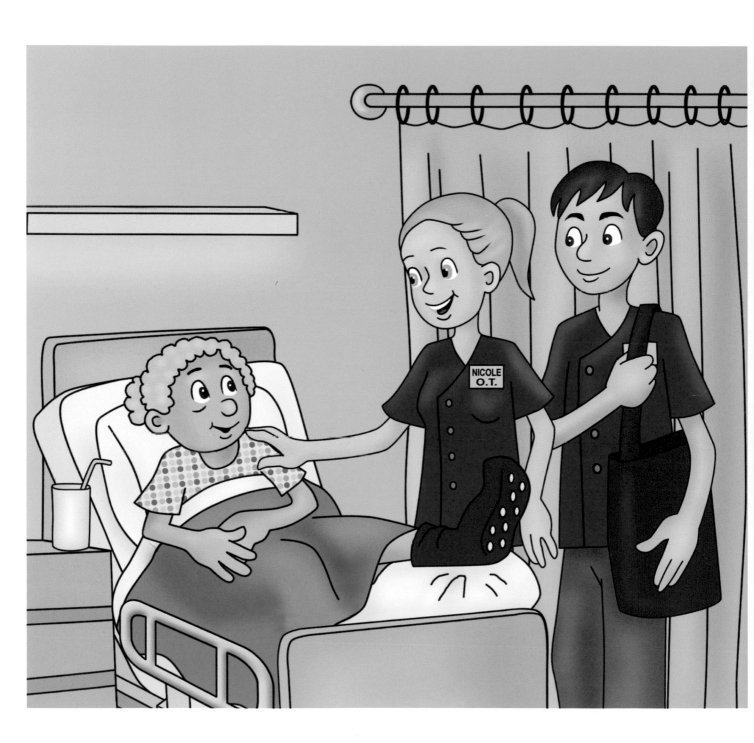

The next day, two very nice people arrived in Yiayia and Papou's hospital room. "We have come to help. We are from rehab."

Papou with his poor hearing said, "No, I did not call a cab."

Yiayia giggled and shouted, "PAPOU YOU NEED TO TURN ON YOUR HEARING AIDS, PLEASE!"

Papou turned on his hearing aids and smiled, "Oh, well hello, you must be the maids."

Yiayia whispered, "Since Papou bumped his head, he has not been the same, not at all."

The two nice people said, "Our names are Ron and Nicole. We are occupational therapists."

Sophia yanked on Nicole's scrub top and asked, "I have never heard of an occupational therapist. Can you explain what that means?"

Nicole said, "We are not doctors or nurses. We are occupational therapists, but you may call us OTs."

Ron explained, "Our job is to help Papou and Yiayia get better in time for the Papadopoulos family Christmas. We will teach them how to get dressed, bake pies, play cards, and more. OTs help people get back to life and do whatever it is that they need to do!"

Yiayia's eyes lit up as she looked at Papou. They both laughed while they tossed their pillows in the air! Dimitrios stood on his hind legs and twirled around and around. Sophia said, "That must be the best news that donkey has heard in a while."

The whole Papadopoulos family shouted, "Opa!"

The OTs had given hope to the whole Papadopoulos family. Yiayia cried, "Occupational therapy sounds wonderful. Tell us what to do."

Nicole told Yiayia, "I have all sorts of adaptive equipment and gadgets. I will teach you how to use them yourself to get bathed and dressed while following hip precautions. These precautions are better known as the rules."

Nicole explained, "If Yiayia bends over or crosses her legs, she could damage her new hip. She would go back to the operating room and have surgery again!" Sophia was surprised that Yiayia was not allowed to bend over to wash her feet or put on her shoes. Nicole gave Yiayia a gadget called a reacher. Sophia saw that it would help her grandmother do those things she couldn't bend to do.

Yiayia nicknamed the reacher her picker-upper and used it to pick up things from the floor so she would not hurt her new hip. Nicole said, "There is also a gadget called a sock aide to put on your socks. I'll also give you a dressing stick to slip off your socks and shoes."

Next, Nicole showed Yiayia how to use a long-handled sponge to wash her toes. The OT had a gadget for everything and Yiayia was beginning to have fun in therapy.

Long Handle Sponge

Reacher

Dressing Stick

Sock Aide

Nicole told Sophia, "Wait until you see the sock puller-upper!"

Yiayia said, "It is the best."

Sophia watched Yiayia put her socks on a piece of plastic and held tight to the two strings on the side. She tossed it over her foot and up she pulled. When her sock was on, her family all exclaimed, "Opa!"

Yiayia worked hard in OT learning how to use all the gadgets and follow the rules. She decided to take a little rest. Before she dozed off, she told Sophia, "If Nicole helps me bake a pie in OT, that will be a very good lesson."

While Yiayia was napping and dreaming of blueberry pie, Papou was working with Ron in OT. Ron was teaching Papou the order to put on his clothes. Papou was puzzled, "Should I put me pants on before me underwear?"

Ron labeled Papou's clothes so he knew what to put on first and what to put on last. This helped Papou know to put on his socks before his shoes.

Sophia stopped by the OT room because she was curious about what Papou was doing. Papou saw Sophia and said, "Hi, Athena? Constance? Uh… Helen? I want to ask you something but me no remember the question."

Sophia was upset that Papou still did not know her name. Ron told her, "After some OT, Papou will remember the Papadopoulos family members." Sophia was trying to be patient. She decided to use this time to try and figure out how to answer Papou's important question.

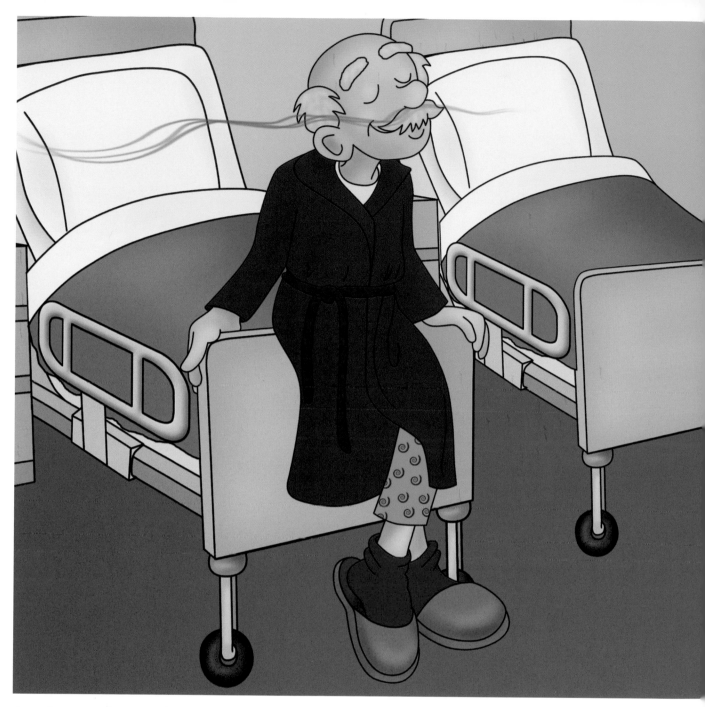

Another week went by and Yiayia was walking around, "I am using a walker with a tray to safely carry things." She stood with her special walker, "Look, Papou! The cards I am dealing!"

Papou tried and tried to play cards with Yiayia, but couldn't remember the game. He said, "Something must have happened to me head in that terrible fall."

Meanwhile, Nicole and Yiayia were in the OT kitchen cooking up an extra-special treat that smelled very good. Papou raised his eyebrows and said, "I smell fresh blueberries." His nose was sniffing and his lips were smacking.

Ron asked Papou, "Who do you think was the cook?"

Papou exclaimed, "Why, it's Yiayia!" He looked at his family and named them, "Sophia! Dimitrios!" After naming each relative correctly, the whole Papadopoulos family shouted, "Opa!"

The OTs had used the smell of the blueberry to trigger Papou's memory. The blueberry pie turned out to be the best gadget of all. That afternoon Papou won the card game! The OTs nodded, "I believe our occupational therapy with Papou and Yiayia is done!"

Dimitrios let out a big donkey sigh, and a tear rolled down his cheek. He was going to miss Ron and Nicole.

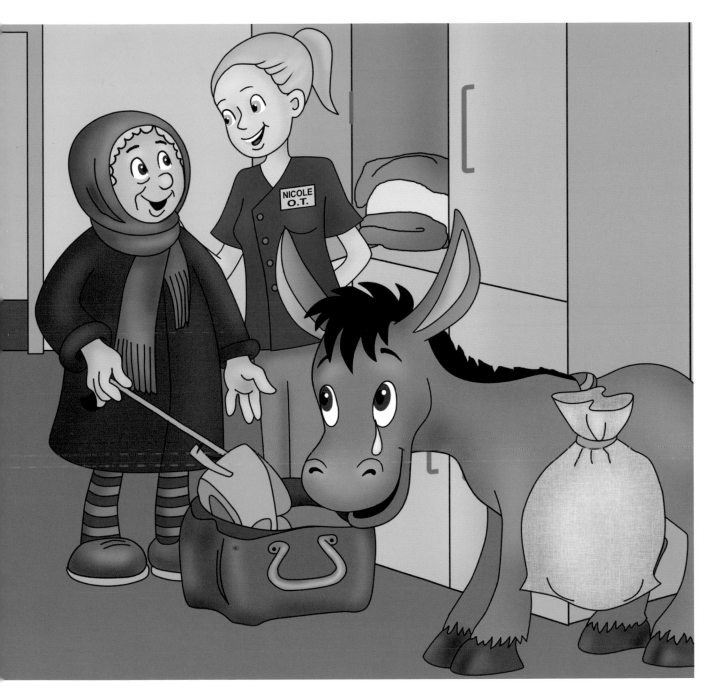

On the last day of OT, Papou got dressed by himself. "I put me shoes on the correct feet. I tucked me shirt in under me sweater vest."

Yiayia moved around the room using her reacher to pack up their clothes. "Oh dear, I'd better load up all my gadgets in Dimitrios' burlap sack so we will be ready to go."

Ron and Nicole gave Papou and Yiayia each a pat on the back, "At last, your hard work in therapy has come to an end. Helping the two of you get better in time for the Papadopoulos Christmas sure made our jobs fun!"

About the Author

Nicole graduated from The Ohio State University and practices occupational therapy in Columbus, Ohio. She enjoys helping people become as independent as possible and wants kids to learn about occupational therapy. It is a rewarding profession with many opportunities. Nicole often writes funny, heart-warming poems for her patients going through rehab. Nicole was inspired to write this story by all the visiting and very curious grandchildren of her patients. Nicole tied her upbringing in the Albanian/Greek communities to mix some culture and fun into this story. Nicole and her husband, Ron, enjoy traveling and value their family and community.